Roll of Thunder, Hear My Cry

by

Mildred B. Taylor

Teacher Guide

Written by:
Anne Troy
and
Joan Primeaux

Note

The Bantam Starfire paperback edition of the book was used to prepare this teacher guide. The page references may differ in the hardcover or other paperback editions.

ISBN 1-56137-085-1

Novel Units

P.O. Box 1461
Palatine, IL 60078

Telephone: (800) 424-2084

Table of Contents

Skills and Strategies

Thinking
Brainstorming, research, synthesizing ideas

Writing
Titling, concept expansion, newspaper article

Vocabulary
Word maps

Comprehension
Predicting, story mapping

Listening/Speaking
Role play

Literary Elements
Character development, simile/metaphor, idioms, foreshadowing

Summary

Cassie Logan and her family are determined not to surrender their independence or to lose their land. Cassie has grown up protected, strong, and unaware that any white person could consider her inferior or to force her to be untrue to herself. But the events of one year turn Cassie's world upside down as she faces being a black among whites.

Initiating Activities

1. Brainstorm the word **segregation** (Activity Sheet 1).

   Rules for brainstorming:

   1. All ideas count
   2. Add details to others' ideas
   3. Adapt others' ideas

2. Make a time line showing:

   a. 1619-The arrival of the first slaves
   b. 1620-The arrival of the Pilgrims
   c. 1775-1783-The Revolutionary War
   d. 1861-1865-The Civil War
   e. 1863-The Emancipation Proclamation
   f. 1930-1935-The Great Depression

Recommended Procedure

This book will be read one section at a time, using DRTA (Directed Reading Thinking Activity) Method. This technique involves reading a section based on what has already occurred in the story. The students continue to read and verify predictions at the end of each section (Activity Sheet 2).

Activity Sheet 1

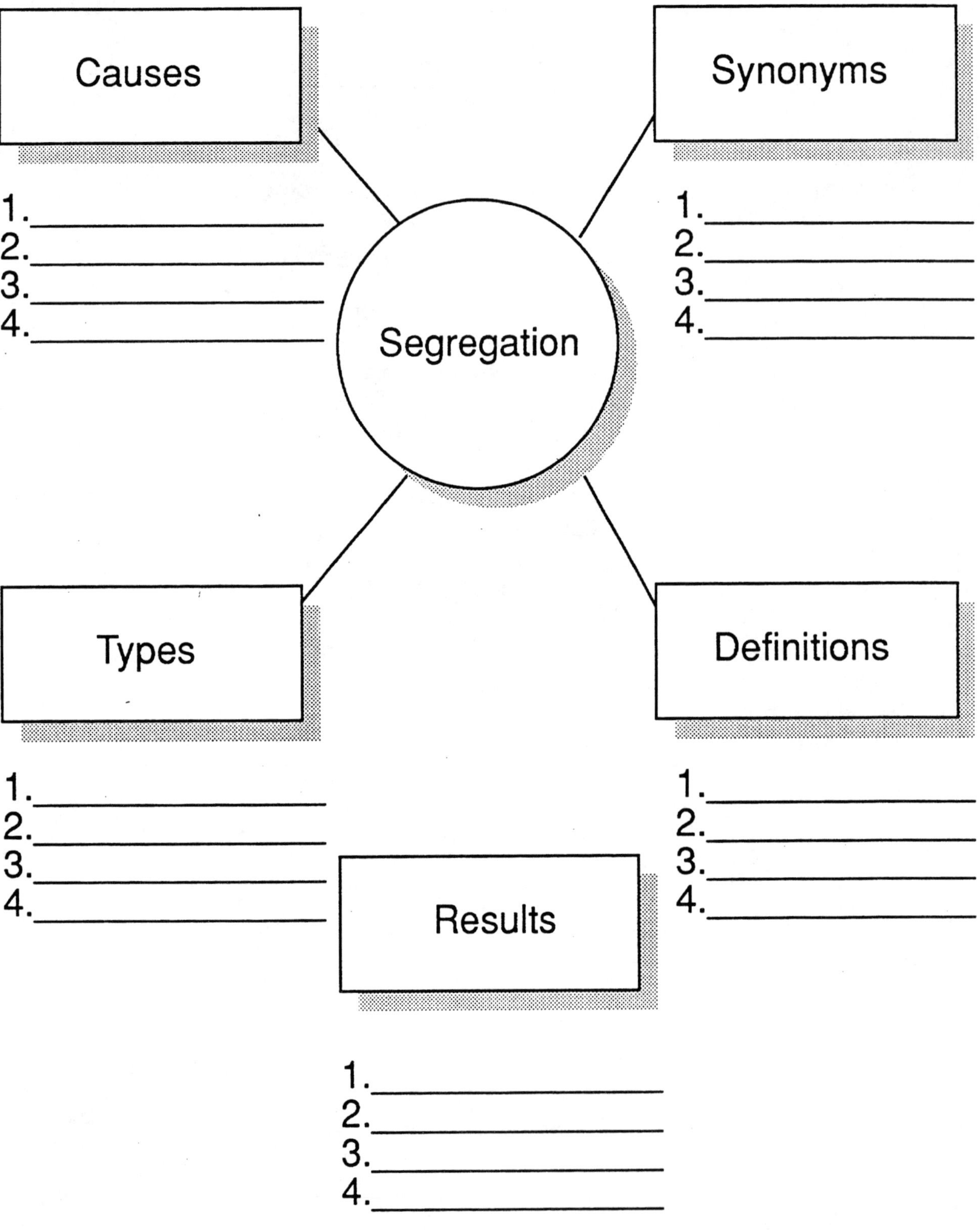

Prediction and Recommended Procedure Sheet

Using Predictions in the Novel Unit Approach:
We all make predictions as we read--little guesses about what will happen next, how the conflict will be resolved, which details given by the author will be important to the plot, which details will help to fill in our sense of a character. Students should be encouraged to predict, to make sensible guesses. As students work on predictions, these discussion questions can be used to guide them: What are some of the ways to predict? What is the process of a sophisticated reader's thinking and predicting? What clues does an author give us to help us in making our predictions? Why are some predictions more likely than others?

A predicting chart is for students to record their predictions. As each subsequent chapter is discussed, you can review and correct previous predictions. This procedure serves to focus on predictions and to review the stories.

Predicting what will happen

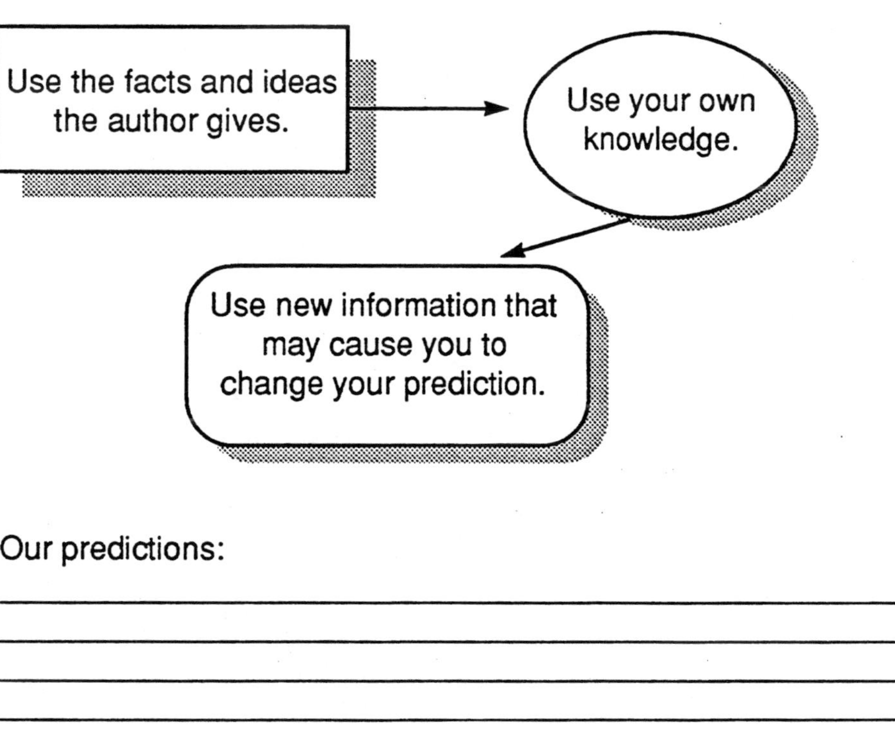

Our predictions:

____

____

____

____

____

Activity Sheet 2

What Characters have we met so far?	What is the conflict in the story?	What are your predictions?	Why did you make those predictions?

Chapter 1
Pages 1-22

Vocabulary

meticulously - p.1	intriguing - p.2	raucous - p.3
sharecropping - p.3	mortgage - p.3	emaciated - p.4
morosely - p.7	amiably - p.7	ridiculed - p.9
temerity - p.16	maverick - p.22	

1. The teacher will read part of the first chapter, pages 1-10, aloud to the class. This helps a class get started with a novel, motivates students, and provides teacher as a model for reading.

2. The students will determine who is telling the story.

3. Locate the setting for the story on a large classroom map. Each student will mark the location of Mississippi on his map. (Activity Sheet 3)

4. Many stories have the same parts---a setting, a problem, a goal, and a series of events that lead to an ending or conclusion. These story elements may be placed on a story map, which like a road map leads a reader from one point to another. There are many different types of story maps. Students may use one of the types included or make up one of their own. (Activity Sheet 4)

   What information do we have to begin a story map?
   - Δ What is the setting?
   - Δ Who is the main character?
   - Δ What is the problem?

5. Begin an attribute web for Cassie. (Activity Sheet 5)

6. Reread paragraph 3 on page 4. What does Papa mean when he says, "You ain't never had to live on nobody's place but your own..."?

7. Why do you think the white school and the black school didn't share the school bus? Find out your school district's policy for providing transportation?

8. Reread paragraph 1 on page 10. Illustrate the Mississippi flag. What is another name for this flag?

9. Why do you think the white school and the black school displayed the flag in a different way?

10. Why is Mama upset with the set of textbooks? *They are old and dirty and the race of the students using the books is marked white and nigra.* What does she do about it? *Mama glues the books shut so the chart with the race does not show.*

Language

Cassie's language is not exactly like our Standard American Dialect. She uses a colloquial or homespun language. A dialect is passed on orally and reflects the vocabulary, usage and pronunciation of a particular region of a country or an ethnic origin, or an occupation.

Background Information on Character for the Teacher

The author may present his characters **directly** or **indirectly.** In direct presentation he tells us straight out what a character is like or has someone else in the story tell us what he is like.

In indirect presentation, the author shows us the character in action; we infer what he is like from what he thinks or says or does.

To be convincing, characterization, must also observe three other principles -- first, characters must be **consistent** in their behavior. They must not behave one way on one occasion and a different way on another unless there is a sufficient reason for change.

Second, characters must be clearly **motivated** in whatever they do, especially when there is any change in behavior.

Third, characters must be **plausible** or **lifelike.**

Change in character:

- Δ must be within the possibilities of character who makes it.
- Δ must be sufficiently motivated by circumstances in which character finds himself.
- Δ must be allowed sufficient time for change to believably take place.

Activity Sheet 3

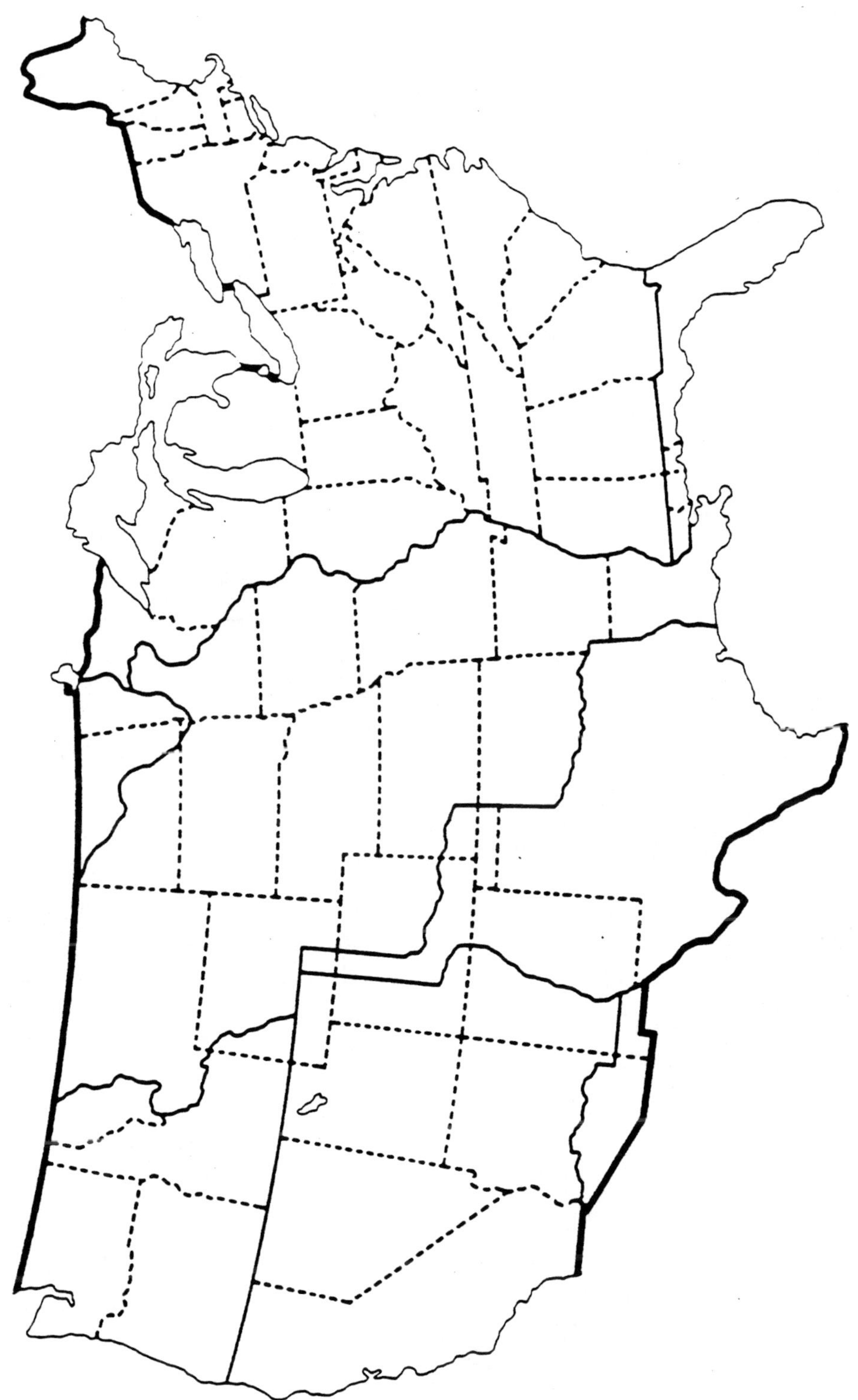

Activity Sheet 4
Story Map Flow Chart

Setting → Problem → Goal → Episodes → Resolution

Setting → Chacters: ________
____
____
____

Problem → Time and Place: ________
____
____

Goal → ________
____
____

Beginning → Development → Outcome

Episodes → ________
____
____
____
____
____
____
____

Resolution → ________
____
____
____
____

Activity Sheet 5

Using Character Attribute Webs

Attribute webs are simply a visual representation of a character from the novel. They provide a systematic way for the students to organize and recap the information they have about a particular character. Attribute webs may be used after reading the novel to recapitulate information about a particular character or completed gradually as information unfolds, done individually, or finished as a group project.

One type of character attribute web uses these divisions:

How a character acts and feels. (How does the character feel in this picture? How would you feel if this happened to you? How do you think the character feels?)

How a character looks. (Close your eyes and picture the character. Describe him to me.)

Where a character lives. (Where and when does the character live?)

How others feel about the character. (How does another specific character feel about our character?)

In group discussion about the student attribute webs and specific characters, the teacher can ask for backup proof from the novel. You can also include inferential thinking.

Attribute webs need not be confined to characters. They may also be used to organize information about a concept or object or place.

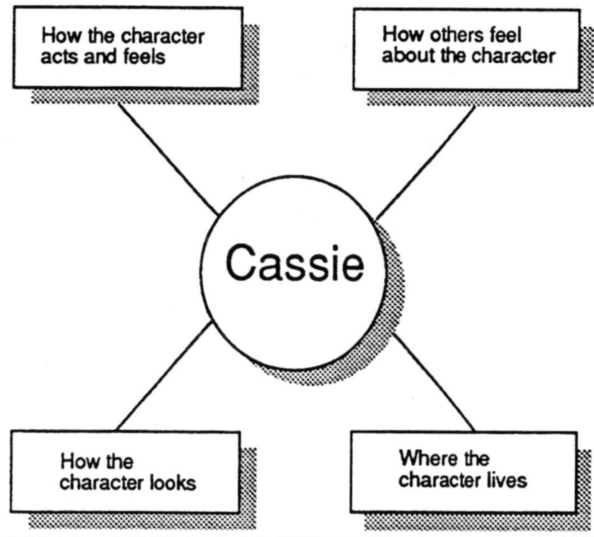

Chapter 2
Pages 23-31

Vocabulary

sinewy - p. 24	ginned - p. 24
formidable - p. 25	penetrating - p. 25
chiffonier - p. 26	congregation - p. 28

The author makes the reader see and feel everything that is happening in the story by using literary techniques. A **Simile** uses the words **like** or **as** to compare two very different things a **Metaphor** suggests a comparison by saying one thing **is** another without using *like* or *as.*

1. What simile is used to describe Mr. Morrison's voice? Does it have anything to do with the title of the book? Keep track of the page numbers where the word thunder is used. *p. 27 "...deep, quiet voice like the roll of low thunder."*

2. Why does Mr. Logan refuse to shop at the Wallace store?

3. Describe Mr. Morrison. Why do you think he's been invited to live with the Logan family?

Writing Activity

Write a newspaper article using the information on page 29 to describe the burning. Make sure to answer: Who, What, When and Where. What will your headline be?

Prediction

Do you think the children will stay away from the Wallaces' store? What could happen?

Chapter 3
Pages 31-51

Vocabulary

resiliency - p. 31	emitted - p. 31
inaccessible - p. 32	humiliation - p. 32
embittered - p. 33	relent - p. 37
conspiratorily - p. 37	stealthily - p. 37
oblivious - p. 38	defiantly - p. 42
gloat - p. 43	engrossed - p. 44

Foreshadowing -- clues or hints that suggest what will happen later. Foreshadowing adds to suspense by giving us just enough clues to keep us guessing about what will happen next.

Personification -- inanimate objects are endowed with human qualities or are represented as possessing human form.

1. Why does the author talk about thunder? Does it mean more or stand for something more than the beginning of a rain storm?

2. Do you think the Logan family's negative attitude toward the school bus is justified? Why or why not?

3. What could the children have done instead of digging the ditch and causing the accident?

4. Why did Mr. Avery visit the Logan family? *p. 45 To warn them there were night riders.*

5. What was Cassie's reaction when she saw the caravan of cars turn around and leave? *p. 50 Waves of sick terror.* What might have happened if the night riders came to the house?

Research The Ku Klux Klan.

Prediction Will the children be punished for digging the ditch?

Chapter 4
Pages 52-76

Vocabulary

riveted - p. 55
ploy - p. 56
engrossed - p. 64
nauseous - p. 65
subtle - p. 66

1. Begin an attribute web for T.J. Whose friend is he? What is a real **friend?**

2. T.J. tells Stacy, "Friends gotta trust each other." What do you think he means by this? What do you think he was doing in Mama's room?

3. Why does Stacey at first resent Mr. Morrison living with them? *p. 59 He thought he could do all the work and was old enough to defend the family.*

4. Why aren't the Wallaces trustworthy? Do you consider T.J. trustworthy?

5. Why did Stacey have the cheat notes? Why didn't he tell where he got them? If you were in Stacey's shoes, what would you have done? *p. 62*

6. Why does Stacey decide to go to the Wallace store? Why do Cassie and her brothers go, too? What could they have done instead?

7. Why did Mama take the children to see Mr. Berry? *p. 74 To see how much pain and suffering the Wallaces caused by setting fire to a man.*

8. Why do you think Mr. Morrison left it up to the children to tell Mama about the fight?

Research

"Tar and feathering" -- company store money
tenant farmers -- 10% - 15% interest

Chapter 5
Pages 77 - 87

Vocabulary

mercantile - p. 81
bland - p. 83
retaliated - p. 85

1. List two incidents in this chapter in which Cassie feels people are being unfair? Do you agree? Why or why not?

2. Make word maps for **prejudice** and **racism.** (An outline is provided below. Use color to distinguish antonyms, synonyms, etc.)

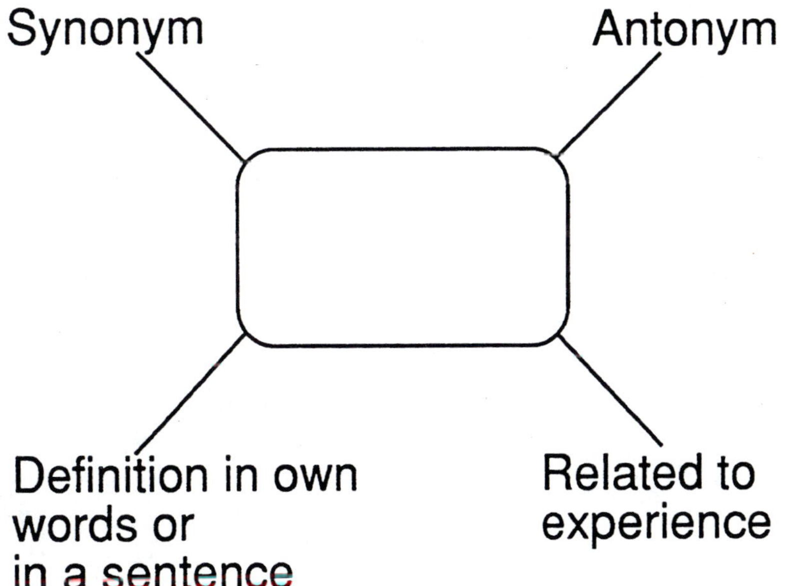

Chapter 6
Pages 88 - 105

Vocabulary

audible - p. 88	mutely - 91	ominously - p. 94
reprimand - p. 94	chignon - p. 98	nape - p. 98
revenge - p. 100	reverently - p. 101	indignant - p. 102
snidely - 103	languidly - p. 104	

1. What do you think would have happened if Uncle Hammer had whipped Simms? *(p. 94)*

2. How does T.J. act when he sees Stacey's new coat? Why does he act like this? Why is Stacey so stupid to give him the coat? *p. 102*

3. What does Uncle Hammer want to do with the Wallaces' store?

Role Play Mr. Morrison talking sense to Uncle Hammer.

Prediction Uncle Hammer made the Wallaces back up their car on the bridge. Mama said, "You shouldn't have done that, Hammer!" What could this foreshadow?

Chapter 7
Pages 106 - 129

Vocabulary

inaudible - p. 107	admonished - p. 107
interminable - p. 109	obnoxiously - p. 109
flaunting - p. 109	wary - p. 112
caldron - p. 114	malevolently - 118
goaded - p. 119	placid - p. 121
candidly - p. 122	insolently - p. 127

1. What is Uncle Hammer trying to teach Stacey?
p. 108 "You care what a lot of useless people say 'bout you you'll never get anywhere; 'cause there's a lotta folks don't want you to make it."

2. What was Uncle Hammer's principle about Stacey's coat?
p. 110 "...a man did not blame others for his own stupidity; he learned from his mistake and became stronger for it."

3. How did Mama react when Stacey told her he gave his new coat away? How would your mother react?

4. What did Papa mean when he said, "Maybe one day whites and blacks can be real friends... The trouble is, down here in Mississippi, it costs too much to find out." *pp. 119-120*

5. How does Cassie feel about T.J.? Are her feelings justified? *pp. 118 - 119*

Chapter 8
Pages 130 - 147

Vocabulary

feigned - p. 132
jovial - p. 135
glade - p. 136
flailed - p. 137
unmercifully - p. 137
banished - p. 138
circumstances - p. 145
testily - p. 146
indignant - p. 146

1. T.J. accuses Cassie of "Uncle Tomming" Lillian Jean. What is an **Uncle Tom** and why would Cassie do this?

2. During his talk with Cassie, Papa says, "...ain't nobody's respect worth more than your own." *p. 134* What does he mean by this?

3. What friendly advice does Cassie give to T.J. about tests?

4. Why does Stacey tell T.J. his family doesn't want to be friends anymore? How does T.J. react? *p. 147*

5. List two reasons Mama got fired. *p. 140 She was teaching about slavery -- things not in the textbook.*

   p. 141 Boycotting shopping at the Wallaces' store.
   - *Shopping in Vicksburg*
   - *Destroyed school property by pasting some pages*

   p. 145 T.J. told all this at the Wallaces' store because Mama failed him because he cheated.

Chapter 9
Pages 148 - 164

Vocabulary

kin - p. 149	amenities - p. 154	chain gang - p. 155
unsympathetic - p. 157	exasperation - p. 158	rile - p. 158
immobilized - p. 160		

1. List three of Papa's character's traits.
   -- strong -- honest
   -- hard-working -- loving father

2. Explain what Papa means: "It's hard on a man to give up, but sometimes it seems there's just ain't nothing else he can do." *pp. 155 - 156*

3. What's the lesson Papa's trying to teach with the comparison of the fig, oak and walnut trees? *p. 156 The little fig tree is like Papa and his family. "...got roots that run deep, and it belongs in the yard as much as that oak and walnut."*

4. Notice the number of times thunder is mentioned in this book? What causes thunder? What other meanings could thunder have?

5. Why did Papa want Stacey to go on the trip to Vicksburg? *p. 157 "I want him to know business... how to take care of it, how to take care of things when I ain't around."*

6. What is foreshadowing? *Clues or hints that suggest what will happen later.* Do you suppose the author is getting us ready for something very sad? *p. 157*

7. Why were the men in the truck shooting at Papa and Mr. Morrison? *p. 163 They had driven to Vicksburg for supplies which made the Wallaces and Mr. Granger angry.*

8. Who are T.J.'s new friends? Cassie doesn't understand why T.J. would be their friend. What does Mama have to say about this? *p. 150-151 "Some folks just like to keep other folks around to laugh at them... use them."*

Prediction

If Papa should die, how would his death affect the family? What would happen to their land and home?

Chapter 10
Pages 165 - 183

Vocabulary

ledger - p. 165	despondently - p. 169
feat - p. 170	mute - p. 171
phenomenal - p. 171	lethargically - p. 172
persistent - p. 173	revival - p. 177
adamantly - p. 179	assurance - p. 181
jauntily - p. 181	condescending - p. 182

1. Why didn't Papa want to write to Uncle Hammer to borrow money? *p. 166 He'd come back angry and get himself hung.*

2. How did Uncle Hammer get the money? *p. 178 Sold his car.* What does that say about Uncle Hammer?

3. List two character traits of Kaleb Wallace. *p. 170 cowardness, prejudiced.*

4. Mildred Taylor describes the heat in August as clinging like an invisible shroud. She writes "... people moved slowly, lethargically, as if under water." What do you think she means by this? *p. 172*

5. What does Stacey hear about T.J.? Why doesn't he tell Jeremy? Would you? Why or why not? *He'd been stealing from Mr. Lanier and running around with white boys.*

Prediction What will happen to T.J.?

Chapter 11
Pages 184 - 195

Vocabulary

frenzied - p. 187
vulnerability - p. 189
emitted - p. 193
placid - p. 193
affirmation - p. 194
despicable - p. 189
interminable - p. 191
prone - p. 193
crescendo - p. 194

1. Make an attribute web for Mr. Jamison. Go back to each chapter where he has been mentioned. What has he stood for in this novel? *A white man who believes in the law.*

2. Why do you think Mr. Morrison had sat on the porch every night since Papa had been injured? Who do you think he had been waiting for? *a lynch mob*

3. Who is to blame for this problem? *T.J.*

4. Why did R.W. and Melvin beat T.J.? *p. 188 T.J. was going to tell that the other two had hurt or maybe killed Mr. and Mrs. Barnett at the breakin.*

5. What kind of a friend is Stacey to T.J.? How does Cassie explain it? *p. 189 "As far back as I could remember, Stacey had felt a responsibility for T.J.... Perhaps he felt that even a person as despicable as T.J. needed someone he could call friend..."*

Chapter 12
Pages 196 - 210

Vocabulary

traipsing - p. 197
menacingly - p. 198
transfixed - p. 200
adamant - p. 203
oblivious - p. 204

1. Although Papa's leg was injured, what does he do as soon as he hears about Stacey and T.J. in the woods? *p. 197*

2. What advice does Mama give Papa as he prepares to leave the house? *p. 197 "Not with the shotgun." p. 198 "Get Harlan Granger to stop it."*

3. What does Mama say is the cause of the fire? *p. 199 lightning* What is the real cause? *p. 198 & 208 Papa set the fire to save T.J. and Stacey.*

4. What does Papa sacrifice in the fire? *His cotton crop.*

Writing Activity

1. Write a different ending to this story. This had an extremely sad ending. Brainstorm other possible endings.

2. Write chapter titles.

Culminating Activities

1. Reports on research on: Ku Klux Klan, share cropping, tar and feathering and tenant farmers.

2. Does this story have a hero? (Activity Sheet 6)
Could this story have more than one hero? Be able to justify your answer with specific page references.

3. Explain the significance of the title. What other titles could you think of for this novel?

4. What was the author's message in this book? What is the most important thing to remember about this story?

5. Summarize the story using the story map. Which type of story map helps most? How would using a story map help you as an author? (Activity Sheet 7)

Activity Sheet 6

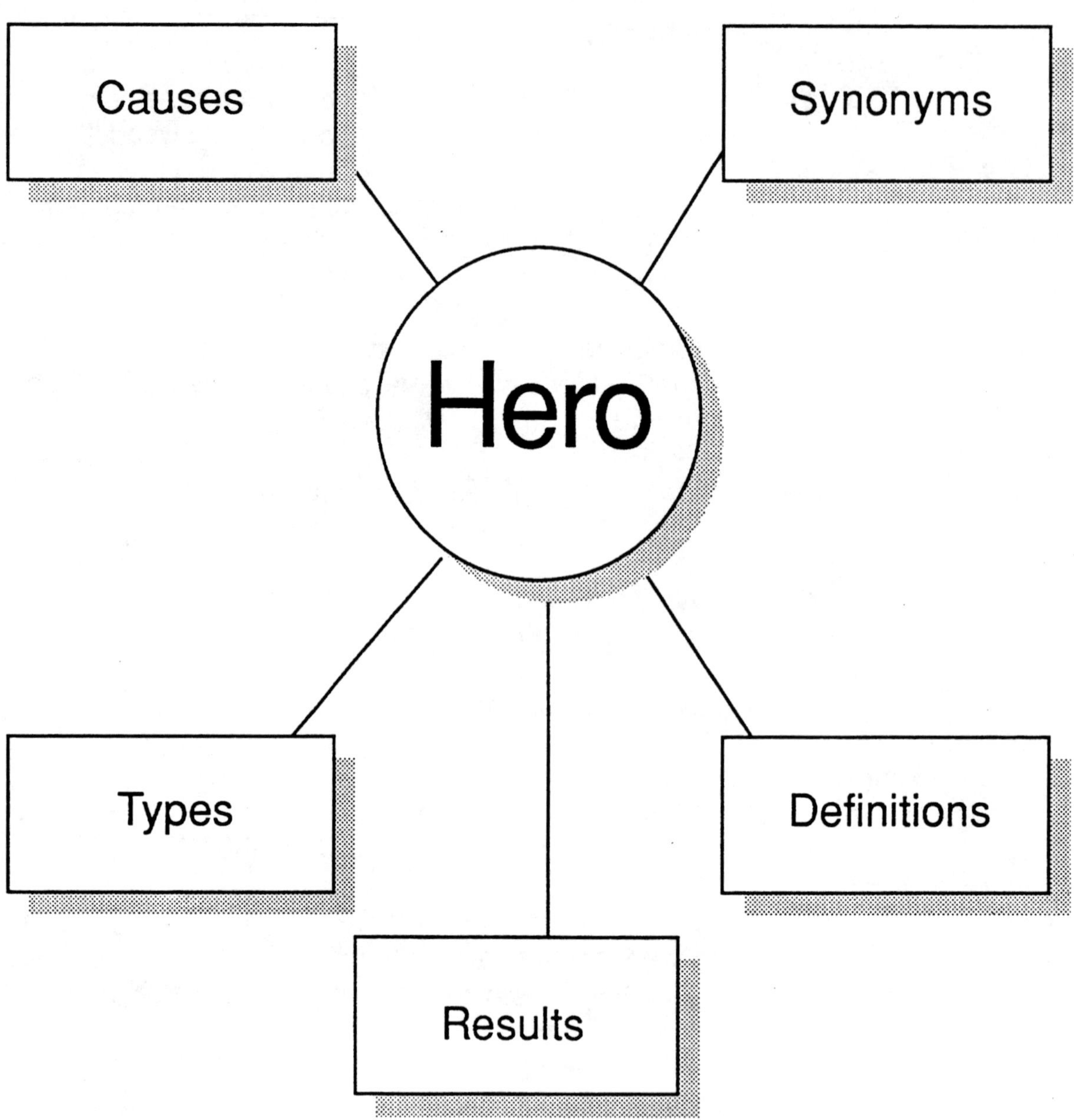

Activity Sheet 7

Story Map

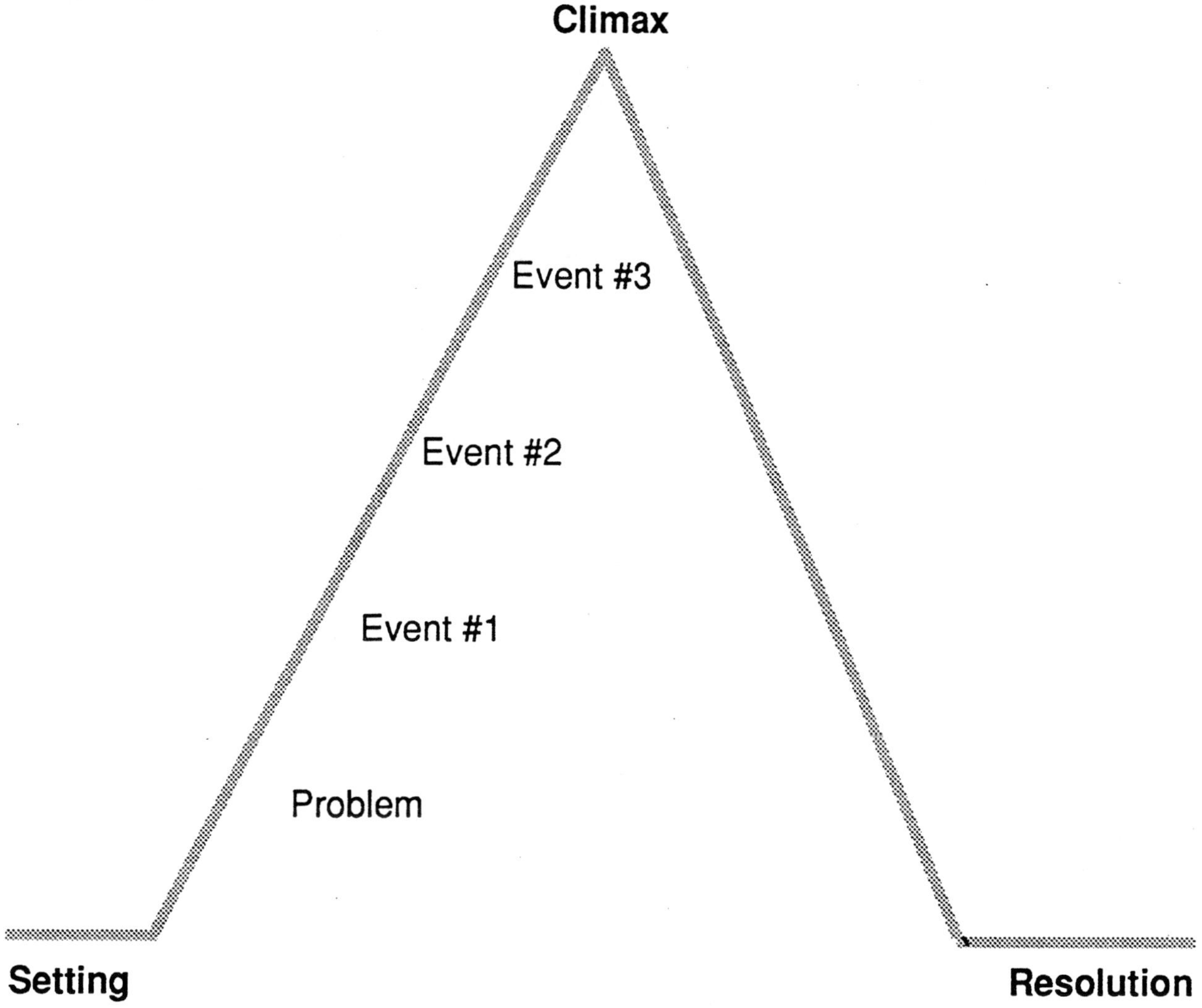

Climax

Event #3

Event #2

Event #1

Problem

Setting

Resolution

Activity Sheet 8

Read each generalization. Then in your own words, list at least **two** pieces of evidence to support it.

Generalizations

1. The Logan family isn't very fond of T.J.
2. The black townspeople aren't treated fairly.
3. The Logan family members are supportive of each other.
4. Papa prefers to use nonviolence when he's provoked.

Generalization	Evidence

Activity Sheet 9

Simile Sometimes an author uses a simile (sim•a•lee) to help the reader form an image.

A simile is a comparison between two things.

A simile uses the words **like** or **as.**

Directions Read the simile in the left column. List the **two** things that are being compared in the right column.

Simile	Objects being compared
1. Before us the narrow, sun-splotched road wound like a lazy serpent dividing the high forest bank of quiet, old trees...	1. road, serpent
2. ...a bus bore down on him spewing clouds of red dust like a huge yellow dragon breathing fire.	2.
3. I squinted, shadowing my eyes from the sun, then slipped like lightning down the pole.	3.
4. When Papa saw us, he began running swiftly, easily, like the wind.	4.
5. ...the tat-tat of the rain against the tin roof changed to a deafening roar that sounded as if thousands of giant rocks were being hurled against the earth.	5.
6. The bus' left front wheel was in our ditch, its right wheel was in the gully, like a lopsided billy goat on its knees.	6.
7. A caravan of headlights appeared suddenly in the east, coming fast along the rain-soaked road like cat eyes in the night.	7.

8. The caravan's seven pairs of rear lights glowing like distant red embers.	8.
9. I could see Mr. Morrison clearly, moving silently, like a jungle cat from the side of the house to the road, a shotgun in his hand.	9.
10. Here it is Saturday morning and the boys are quiet as church mice.	10.
11. Stacey tore across the Wallace yard and, leaping high like a forest fox, fell upon T.J., knocking him down.	11.
12. Paul Edward had himself a mind like a steel trap.	12.
13. When I rejoined Mama she was combing her hair, which fanned her hair like an enormous black halo.	13.
14. The night men swept down like locusts.	14.
15. Uncle Hammer wore, as he had every day since he had arrived, sharply creased pants, a vest over a snow-white shirt, and shoes that shone like midnight.	15.
16. Lillian Jean was grinning like a Cheshire cat.	16.
17. Sweat popped off Mr. Morrison's skin like oil on water.	17.
18. Mr. Morrison set the truck down as gently as a sleeping child.	18.
19. People moved slowly through the heat as if underwater.	19.
20. The branches of the trees met like long green fans sheltering us.	20.

Activity Sheet 10

Metaphor Sometimes an author uses a metaphor (met•a•for) to help the reader form an image.

A **metaphor** is a comparison between two unlike objects.

Example The man was a human tree in height.

What two things are being compared?

Metaphor	Objects being Compared
1. Our faces were eager question marks. Translation: (Your own words)	1.
2. ...the dust swelled up in rolls of billowing clouds behind us. Translation:	2.
3. The night whispered of distant thunder. Translation:	3.

Activity Sheet 11

Idioms

An **idiom** is a group of words whose meaning must be known as a whole.

Example

"To go back on your word."
This doesn't mean "To back up on your word."
It means, "To change your mind."

An **idiom** is also the language used by the people of a certain region or group.

Example

"Hi, you guys!" (an American idiom)

Mildred Taylor, **Roll of Thunder, Hear My Cry's** author uses some idioms which may be confusing.

Idiom	Translation (your own words)
1. But Mama, that Lillian Jean ain't got the brains of a flea.	1.
2. I was beginning to think Mr. Simms was a bit touched in the head.	2.
3. My temper almost flew out of my mouth.	3.
4. The friendship with Lillian Jean had all been a game.	4.
5. (Write your own Idiom for #5)	5.